Beep Beep Bubbie

For Zoe, who inspired the story. For Toma and Aaron, who beeped.
And for Michael, who keeps my batteries charged—BSK

To Jean-Christophe, always there to support me —ÉEP

Text copyright © 2020 by Bonnie Sherr Klein · Illustrations copyright © 2020 by Élisabeth Eudes-Pascal

LIBRARY AND ARCHIVES CANADA CATALOGUING IN PUBLICATION

Title: Beep beep Bubbie / Bonnie Sherr Klein ; illustrations by Élisabeth Eudes-Pascal.
Names: Klein, Bonnie Sherr, author. | Eudes-Pascal, Élisabeth, illustrator.
Identifiers: Canadiana 20200244930 | ISBN 9781926890234 (hardcover)
Classification: LCC PS8621.L43 B44 2020 | DDC jC813/.6—dc23

Book design by Elisa Gutiérrez
The text of this book is set in IM FELL Great Primer. Title is set in Oyster
Printed and bound in Canada on forest-friendly paper.

MIX
Paper from responsible sources
FSC
www.fsc.org
FSC® C016245

10 9 8 7 6 5 4 3 2 1

The publisher thanks the Government of Canada, the Canada Council for the Arts and Livres Canada Books for their financial support. We also thank the Government of the Province of British Columbia for the financial support we have received through the Book Publishing Tax Credit program and the British Columbia Arts Council.

Beep Beep Bubbie

Bonnie Sherr Klein

illustrations by Élisabeth Eudes-Pascal

TRADEWIND BOOKS
Vancouver · London

I t was *Shabbat*—the Jewish Sabbath—the day Kate and her
little brother Nate spent with their grandmother, Bubbie.
I can't wait to show Bubbie this library book, Kate thought.
"Bubbie is taking us to Granville Island to buy apples for Rosh
Hashanah," she told Nate. "And she has a surprise for us!"

"Surprise!" Bubbie shouted from her new scooter as
Kate and Nate arrived. Luna ran beside, wagging her tail.
"Arf! Arf!" barked Luna.
"Beep-beep," sounded the scooter.

"BEEP BEEP," said Nate, pressing the horn.
"What do you think of my new scooter, Kate?"
A scooter? That was the surprise?
"Everything will be different now," Kate said glumly.
"Maybe different is good," Bubbie said. "Long ago,
people who had trouble walking were stuck indoors."

Kate was still upset. She already missed the Bubbie
she used to have. That Bubbie danced and took them
to climate marches.

"Would you like a ride on my scooter?" offered Bubbie.

"No, not now, Bubbie. Maybe later. What fun can we have on a scooter anyway?"

"Lots of fun!"

"But how can we get to Granville Island?"

"Simple. We take the bus. It has a ramp for us."

"Honk! Honk!" tooted the bus as it lowered the ramp.

"Scooter coming on!" announced the driver. "Everyone, move back, please!"

"So, *we* have to get out of the way?" one man grumbled as he got up to move.

"This is going to take all day!"

"Beep-beep," went the scooter.
"BEEP BEEP," Nate joined in.
In no time, Bubbie backed into a tricky space behind a pole.
"OK, driver, brakes are on! Ready to go!"

"These apples are really heavy," Kate complained.

"Not for my scooter." Bubbie smiled.

Soon grocery bags piled up in the scooter basket and on the handlebars.

Whoops! Nate tripped and fell. He started to cry.

Kate tried to comfort him, but Nate kept crying.

So she plopped him up on Bubbie's lap. "Here, Bubbie, you take Nate."

Bubbie rocked and sang to him. "Shhhh, shhh."

Nate stopped crying.

Kate was impressed. Bubbie was still Bubbie, even on the scooter.

"Arf! Arf!" Luna barked from the backpack.

"Uh-oh, we'd better get Luna to the park," said Kate.

"Luna, fetch!" Kate threw a ball.
Two kids joined in the fun.

"I'm Catherine, and this is Omar," said the girl.
"Hi, I'm Kate," said Kate.

Then Luna pooped.
"Gross!" exclaimed Kate.

"That's OK, I can *scoot* the poop!" said Bubbie.
She leaned over her scooter, scooped Luna's poop
into a baggie, and scooted it right to the garbage bin.

Bubbie took out a kite from her backpack.
In a moment, it was flying high in the
sky above the city.

"Your grandma is so cool!" Catherine shouted out to Kate.

Back at Bubbie's garden, Kate picked some flowers
and put them in the scooter's basket. "Your scooter's
a good friend, Bubbie. I think it needs a name."

"Great idea, Kate. Any suggestions?"

"How about Gladys!"

"Gladys?" asked Bubbie.

Kate pulled out the library book she'd
brought along and handed it to Bubbie.

FRANCES WILLARD

WOMEN
CAN
DO
ANYTHING
AND
GIRLS
TOO!

Over a hundred years ago Frances Willard fought for women to have the right to vote. When Frances was 53 years old, she learned to ride a bicycle to show that women could do anything.

"Women didn't ride bikes then?" Kate asked. "Why?"

"People were afraid women's ankles would show under their petticoats. Can you believe it?"

Kate rolled her eyes. "Or maybe their underpants might show!" They all laughed!

Kate read the book aloud over Bubbie's shoulder: *Frances Willard named her bicycle Gladys because riding a bike made her heart glad.*

"Gla-a-a-d," sang Nate.

"And you seem glad riding on your new scooter, Bubbie," said Kate. "Can we decorate Gladys? Please?"

Kate painted colourful patterns and the name
Gladys on the scooter. Nate added his handprint.

"I think I'm ready for that ride now, Bubbie," said Kate.

"Beep-beep!" Kate pressed the horn as they drove in circles.
"BEEP BEEP," echoed Nate.
Together they sang out, "BEEP BEEP, BUBBIE!"

Soon Kate and Nate were off to many
new adventures with Bubbie and Gladys . . .